Tara kiranam

-Gayathri Reddy Yellamula

Tara Kiranam
© 2025 Gayathri
All rights reserved.

No part of this publication may be reproduced, stored, or transmitted in any form or by any means—electronic, mechanical, photocopying, recording, or otherwise—without the prior written permission of the publisher or author.

This is a work of fiction. Names, characters, places, and incidents are products of the author's imagination or are used fictitiously. Any resemblance to actual events, locales, or persons, living or dead, is purely coincidental.

First Edition
Published in India by Notion Press
www.notionpress.com

<u>Dedication</u>

To every woman who has waited in
silence.
To every couple who found home in each
other, even without answers.
And to the quiet strength that love can be.

-Gayathri

<u>Acknowledgements</u>

Writing Tara Kiranam was not just a creative journey, but a deeply personal one.

To my family — thank you for your love and unwavering belief in me.

To every reader walking through silence, longing, and reconnection — may this story remind you that you are not alone.

And to those who carry the weight of unspoken dreams — this story is for you.

-Gayathri

Table of content :

Chapter 1

The Echo of Goodbye

The platform was crowded, but Tara felt alone in the chaos.

Metal wheels screeched against rusted tracks as the train pulled in, a slow giant arriving to tear something away. People bustled around with luggage and loud goodbyes, but Tara and Kiran stood silently near the bench under the flickering LED board that read: Train 12601 – Departure 06:35 AM.

It wasn't their first goodbye — but somehow, it felt heavier.

Tara adjusted the strap of her handbag, trying to focus on anything but his eyes. They had moved to this city three years ago, chasing stability in Kiran's IT career. Back then, it had felt like an adventure. A new city. A new apartment. Late-night dosas from roadside stalls. But over time, the city had become a place of echoing silences — especially when Kiran worked long hours and Tara waited alone for dinner.

Now, a job offer had come. A teaching post in her hometown — the kind she had once dreamed of. Close to her parents. Familiar lanes. Her own rhythm again. It should have felt like a win. But standing here, on this station soaked in early morning chill, she wasn't sure what she was walking towards — or away from.

Kiran cleared his throat. "Call me… once you reach."

She nodded. "I will."

The train horn cut through the air, urgent and impatient.

He stepped forward, gently took her suitcase, and placed it near the train door. Then, he stood back, hands in his jacket pockets. That was the thing with Kiran — he was always careful with luggage, but never with words.

Tara hesitated before boarding. A part of her wanted him to say something that would make her stay. Or maybe just something… anything… to show her that this mattered. That her leaving would leave a space in his day.

But instead, he looked at his watch.

"I should get to the cab. Office call at nine," he said, not meeting her eyes.

She forced a smile. "Yeah. Don't be late."

As the train began to move, she stood by the door for a few seconds longer, watching him shrink into the crowd. He didn't wave. Neither did she.

But long after the platform disappeared from sight, Tara still felt the weight of what was left unsaid. The silence between them had grown roots — quiet, invisible, and far too deep.

She pulled out her phone and opened a blank note.

"The echo of goodbye isn't loud. It's the silence after that stays."

She typed, then stared at it, unsure if it was a thought or just the truth.

The train moved forward.

And so did she.

Or at least, she hoped she would.

Chapter 2

Threads of Routine

The scent of old books and floor disinfectant filled the staff room. Tara sat at her desk, her ID card still flipping lightly in the breeze from the ceiling fan. Around her, teachers discussed syllabi, students, and salary delays. But her mind wandered — to a kitchen two states away, where she once brewed coffee for two.

Her new job was stable, noble even. A quiet government school tucked behind neem trees and uneven roads. She taught English to high schoolers who still folded their notebooks like prayer hands. The work was honest. But the days were eerily quiet.

Every morning, Tara woke up to the sound of temple bells from the street. She'd make her own tea, set out her sari, and walk to school with the same steadiness she once admired in her mother. But with every tick of the clock, she felt the distance grow—not just between cities, but between lives once shared.

Kiran, too, had slipped back into routine. Morning meetings. Evening codes. A dinner photo sent on WhatsApp. Their conversations had become digital —

pixelated greetings, emojis without emotion, and delayed "good nights" that didn't carry warmth anymore.

One night, after school corrections and a quiet dinner of upma, Tara sat on her balcony with a small diary. The moonlight stretched across the railing, soft and silver, and the crickets filled the silence Kiran used to.

She began to write.

> Day 17 — Back home, but not home.

Kiran messaged "take care" today. It felt more like a notification than a sentence.

I don't know when we became polite strangers.

In another city, Kiran leaned back on his office chair, staring at a blank chat window with her name on it. He typed:

"How was school?"

…paused…

…and erased it.

Instead, he sent a thumbs-up on her forwarded staff group photo.

Their lives had become timelines that didn't overlap. Like two trains running on parallel tracks—close, but never meeting.

That weekend, Tara got a call from an old friend. There was a laugh in her voice Tara hadn't heard in a long time. After the call ended, Tara didn't go back to her diary. She just sat there, the page open, pen resting between her fingers.

Maybe some words didn't need paper. Maybe they needed to be spoken — but to whom?

She picked up her phone, saw Kiran's name, stared at it…

…and locked the screen again.

The threads of routine were holding her together — but also slowly weaving a wall.

Chapter 3

Rain Between Us

The drizzle began sometime after dusk. The sky outside Tara's window was a pale blue, fading into grey, and the soft patter of rain tapped against the old glass like a metronome of memory.

Inside her modest flat, Tara sat cross-legged on the floor, a half-knitted woolen scarf lying abandoned in her lap. Her tea had gone cold, untouched. The TV was on mute. And yet, the noise in her mind refused to quiet down.

Her phone vibrated on the table. She didn't need to check it. She already knew what it was.

Another photo. Another cricket stadium. Another caption from Kiran.

" Last-minute pass. What a match!"

She stared at the image. Floodlights shining. Crowd roaring. Kiran grinning ear to ear, surrounded by colleagues. There was so much joy in his face.

And none of it was hers.

She didn't reply.

It wasn't the first time. Cricket had always been Kiran's escape — his comfort zone, his thrill, his weekend religion. Tara had admired that about him once. The way his eyes lit up at a six, the way he remembered old match stats better than their wedding anniversary date.

But now, every match he attended felt like another reminder: of her empty weekends, her unanswered texts, and the quiet dinners eaten with only the sound of cutlery.

She messaged:

Tara: Enjoy. Don't forget dinner.

He didn't respond. Not until past midnight.

Kiran: Just got home. What a game! Dhoni was on fire!

She stared at the message. Then at the rain.

Anger rose in her—not loud, but deep. Not fiery, but aching. Like a familiar wound that had just been pressed again.

She typed quickly:

Tara: I don't remember the last time you sounded this excited about us.

Sometimes I feel you have more love for cricket than for your wife.

Seconds passed.

Then minutes.

Then the "typing…" indicator vanished.

He didn't reply.

Tears stung her eyes—not from the fight, but from how small she felt in his world. Like a line in the margins of his story. Always present, never highlighted.

She threw her phone aside and walked to the balcony. The rain had grown heavier now, pouring like it too was tired of holding back. She stood there, arms wrapped around herself, watching the storm blur the streetlights.

Behind her, the TV flickered. Highlights of a cricket match played on mute.

She went back inside and opened her journal.

> "Some people chase stadium lights.

Some just want to be seen in the dark.

Tonight, I sat in both."

The doorbell didn't ring. The phone didn't buzz again. Just the sound of rain, and her breath trying not to break.

Far away, Kiran sat with his phone in hand. He'd read her message more than once. He wanted to reply. Wanted to explain.

But the match had been his escape—and now guilt was his silence.

He opened her photo. One she had sent days ago. Her in a yellow kurti, smiling with a bunch of students. He remembered when she used to smile like that with him.

He sighed.

Outside his window too, it was raining.

Chapter 4

The Past We Forgot

It began with burnt rice.

Tara had stood in their tiny newlywed kitchen, smoke curling up from the steel pressure cooker. She was barefoot, flustered, and dangerously close to tears. The masoor dal had boiled over. The salt in the curry was missing. And the chapati dough looked more like wet clay than anything edible.

Kiran peeked in from the living room, towel slung across his shoulder. "Babe," he said, trying not to laugh, "are we having a campfire for dinner?"

Tara turned, hands on hips, cheeks flushed. "This is harder than it looks!"

That night, they ordered biryani. And ate it sitting on the floor, laughing between bites, while watching old comedy clips on her laptop.

He taught her slowly—how to feel the texture of the dough, how cumin crackles when it's ready, how to time the whistle of the pressure cooker just right. Tara had never cooked a full meal before marriage. Now, the kitchen was their little universe. Music playing from Kiran's old phone. Spices lined like soldiers on the rack. Laughter seasoning the air.

Their nights were sacred.

They would sit on their small balcony with two cups of coffee, legs brushing under the table. Conversations flowed—about everything and nothing. Politics. Childhood memories. What kind of house they wanted one day. Whether they'd have a dog or two kids. Or both.

Tara used to fall asleep mid-sentence, sometimes with her head on Kiran's shoulder, phone in hand, a smile still on her lips. He'd carefully put the phone away, adjust the pillow, and whisper, "Good night, madam," before turning off the light.

Back then, even the silences between them were warm.

They'd fight, yes. Over unpaid bills. Wet towels on the bed. Forgotten birthdays. But the makeup was always immediate—through hugs, kisses, or warm idlis for breakfast with extra chutney.

Now, sitting alone in her hometown apartment, Tara found herself staring at an old photograph in her gallery.

She and Kiran, in their first apartment. She was wearing his oversized t-shirt, grinning with a spoon in hand, hair tied messily. He was standing behind her, arms around her waist, both of them laughing at a mess she'd made on the kitchen counter.

The Image felt like a postcard from a time when love didn't feel so complicated.

She touched the screen gently, then locked the phone.

That night, she lit a small lamp in the puja room. Sat cross-legged. Closed her eyes.

> ➤ "I miss the version of us that didn't need fixing," she whispered, almost like a prayer.

"I miss the laughter. I miss the 'us' we were before we forgot how to be 'us'."

And in another city, Kiran scrolled through his phone too.

He stopped at a voice note—an old one Tara had sent months ago.

Her voice chirped through the speaker:

"I burnt the curry again, but I swear the rotis are round this time! Come soon, okay?"

Kiran smiled, a small ache blooming in his chest. He listened to it twice. Then closed his eyes.

Sometimes the past doesn't just hurt. It also heals—by reminding you of who you were, and what you once meant to each other.

And sometimes, remembering is the first step toward returning.

Chapter 5

The Unsent Letters

The diary was plain—brown, leather-bound, and neatly tucked into the second drawer of Tara's bedside table.

No one knew it existed. Not even Kiran.

She had started writing in it a few weeks after moving back to her hometown. At first, it was just to keep track of her thoughts, like journaling. But slowly, the entries turned into letters.

Letters she never sent.

"Dear Kiran,

You smiled today. On that video call. When I told you I saw our favorite chocolate in the store, the one we used to fight over. I don't know why, but I felt like crying after the call ended. Maybe because you smiled so easily… and I didn't know if it was for me or just the memory."

– Tara

In a folder named "Voice Drafts" on Kiran's phone, there were seven recordings.

All unsent.

He had started making them on nights when sleep felt foreign. When guilt curled into his chest and loneliness felt heavier than work pressure. He'd talk to the darkness, as if she were beside him again, listening.

"Hey...

It's 1:43 AM. I know you're probably asleep. I miss you. I miss our fights. Even the way you'd glare at me while chopping onions. The house feels quiet. Too quiet. And this time, I don't want cricket or deadlines or anything else to distract me. Just you. I want... I want us again."

– Deleted.

Tara wrote on evenings when the city felt too small, and her heart felt too big. She used ink pens, afraid that typing would make the words feel less personal.

"Dear Kiran,

Do you know I still cook extra? Out of habit.
I set two plates. I delete one text before
sending another. I measure my days by your
replies.

Sometimes I wonder if we'd still be happy if
we hadn't moved apart. But maybe distance
didn't create the gap. Maybe we did."

– Tara

Kiran never played his voice drafts twice.
He'd record, listen once, then delete.
Always halfway between wanting her to
hear, and being too afraid she would.

"Tara..."

(Long pause)

"Sometimes I feel like I failed you. Like I
chose everything else above you. I didn't
mean to. I just... kept assuming you'd
always wait."

– Deleted.

One night, Tara's pen paused.

She turned a page and wrote slowly,
deliberately.

"Dear Kiran,

Maybe one day, I'll read these letters to you.
Or maybe you'll find them by accident, after
I've stopped writing them. But until then,
I'll keep placing parts of me here—quiet,
safe, unseen.

Because even if you can't hear me, I need to
remember that my voice still exists."

– Love, Tara

Somewhere else, Kiran opened his voice
app, hesitated, and closed it again.

He stared at their wedding photo on the
wall. Their smiles frozen in time. A different
version of themselves.

He whispered softly, to no one:

"Goodnight, Tara."

And the night kept their secrets.

Chapter 6

Shadows at the Door

The morning light danced softly on the freshly mopped floor. A faint aroma of sandalwood and filter coffee floated through the air. Tara stood in the kitchen, tying her hair loosely with a clip, her face flushed from the warmth of the stove.

The tiny bangles jingled from the other room.

"Ammaaaa!" a small voice squealed, followed by the sound of little feet running across the tiles.

Tara turned instantly, smiling as her son dashed in, his kurta halfway tucked, mango pulp smeared near his lips.

"Slow down!" she laughed, catching him mid-run. "Where's your Na?"

"He's cutting watermelon! He said no to chocolates again," the boy huffed, frowning.

She chuckled and kissed his forehead. "He's right, my little tiger. Too many sweets, and we'll have to take you to the doctor."

The boy grinned mischievously and ran back toward the living room.

Tara wiped her hands on a towel and peeked into the dining area. Kiran was setting the table, his sleeves rolled up, his face still glowing from a shared inside joke.

"I told you not to let him see the chocolates," Tara said with mock annoyance.

Kiran shrugged, smiling. "I hid them behind the salt container. He has sixth sense, I swear."

They laughed. The sound filled the house like music.

Later, they sat together on the swing in the balcony, the child asleep on Tara's lap. A soft breeze rustled through the trees. Their fingers touched lightly—an old, familiar rhythm.

Kiran looked at her, his voice hushed. "I'm happy, Tara."

She smiled back. "Me too."

The air was thick with peace. With wholeness. With everything that had once felt so far away now sitting quietly beside them.

The kind of day you never want to end.

The kind of love that doesn't need words.

She leaned her head on Kiran's shoulder, her hand gently stroking her son's hair.

For the first time in a long time, she felt full.

Whole.

Safe.

Loved.

Then…

A sound.

A ceiling fan humming.

Tara's eyes fluttered open.

Her pillow was damp. Her arm was numb.

She was alone.

The bed was unmade on only one side. The walls were silent. The aroma of filter coffee

had been nothing but memory. The child—
her child—wasn't real.

She sat up slowly, her chest heavy with the
weight of joy that had just been stolen by
truth.

She walked to the kitchen, poured a glass of
water, and drank quietly, as if mourning
something only she had met.

No tears fell. Not immediately. The silence
itself was too sacred, too full.

But as she lay back down, facing the ceiling
fan spinning in slow circles, one single tear
slid down her cheek.

> She had dreamed of her whole life.

And just like that, morning had taken it
away.

Chapter 7

A Stranger's Kindness

It was a Sunday morning. The city was quiet, lazy with weekend stillness.

Tara sat on the edge of her bed, hair messy from sleep, her fingers wrapped around a lukewarm cup of tea. She hadn't spoken much that morning. Not to herself. Not to anyone.

Then the call came.

Kiran.

The screen blinked.

She answered.

"Hey," his voice came, rough from just waking up. "Did I wake you?"

"No... I've been up," she replied, her tone softer than usual.

He noticed it. He always did.

"Your voice... something's off. Did you cry?" he asked gently.

Tara paused. Her throat tightened. She hated how easily he could see through her, even across miles.

"I had a dream," she said, trying to sound casual.

"What kind of dream?"

She hesitated, then let the words flow. "We were at home. Our home. And… we had a baby. A little boy. He was running around, and you were making watermelon juice for him. He called me 'Amma', Kiran. And I... I felt like I had everything I ever wanted."

Silence on the other end. Only the sound of his breath.

Then, softly, he whispered, "And you woke up to find it wasn't real."

That broke her.

A tear slid down Tara's cheek. "I held him, Kiran. I smelled his skin. I felt it."

Kiran exhaled slowly. "Tara... if dreams can feel that real, imagine how it'll be when it is real. I know it's hard. But we're not done, Tara. You and I — we're still in this."

Her voice cracked. "But what if it never happens?"

"Then we'll adopt the loudest, messiest kid in the world and blame each other for it," he joked.

She laughed, through tears. "He'll have your obsession with cricket and my mood swings. Dangerous combo."

"He'll cry when India loses and scream for biryani when he's sad. Basically… me."

She giggled. He joined.

That familiar warmth returned — their laughter, unfiltered, like the good old nights. For a moment, the ache faded. They were just two people, in love, dreaming again.

"Tara," Kiran said, "you're not alone in this. You've never been. I may not be great at saying it, but... when you're hurting, I feel it here." He tapped his chest. "I'm sorry if I haven't been showing up the way you need."

Tara closed her eyes. "You're here now."

A pause. Then:

"Remember the time you tried to make upma for the first time?" he grinned.

"Don't start," she warned, laughing.

"It was a crime against humanity. Even the gas stove protested."

"Fine! But who taught me to make rasam like your Amma?"

"You did learn," he smiled. "And your rasam's better now. Just don't tell Amma I said that."

That Sunday, they stayed on the call longer than they had in weeks. They talked about small things. Silly things. Kiran teased her about her blanket obsession. She teased him about the way he still said "zebra" like a British kid.

For a while, they weren't a couple struggling with pain.

They were just Tara and Kiran — two people who still loved each other, even in the pauses.

Before hanging up, he said, "Let's name our future baby... something strong."

"Like?"

"Arjun. Or Maya, if it's a girl. Both names for warriors."

Tara smiled. A full smile this time. "Then we better be warriors too, Mr. Cricket Crazy."

"Oh, I am. And you? You're the fiercest woman I know. Don't let a dream make you forget that."

That night, Tara looked at the mirror. Same tired eyes. Same quiet room.

But her heart? It was warmer.

> Sometimes, the stranger you're looking for is just the version of someone you forgot still sees you.

And sometimes, all it takes is a Sunday call to remember that love hasn't gone anywhere.

Chapter 8

When We Forgot Us

The Sunday call lingered.

For a while, everything felt lighter — the tea tasted warmer, the breeze through the window gentler. Tara smiled to herself that evening, the way she hadn't in weeks. She replayed parts of the conversation in her head as she folded laundry and hummed an old melody they used to sing on road trips.

Kiran's voice still echoed in her ears — the jokes, the reassurance, the names for their imaginary children. It was a good day.

But good days don't always last, do they?

By midweek, the quiet crept back in.

Calls became shorter again — not intentionally, just swallowed by work calls, missed alarms, and never-ending to-do lists. Tara texted a few times, but replies came with gaps. Kiran had client meetings, site visits, a presentation he was too anxious about.

She understood. But something inside her… wilted.

One evening, while organizing the bookshelf, she found an old notebook — the one they used to call their "us book." It had silly drawings, recipes they never tried, notes like "Don't forget to cuddle" and "Movie night, even if we fight."

She sat down on the floor, back against the bed, and flipped through it.

A scribbled page in Kiran's handwriting read:

> ➢ "One day we'll be old and grumpy, and I'll still ask you to make tea just so I

can hug you from behind while you roll your eyes."

Tara smiled, then teared up.

When had they stopped writing in this book?

When had their promises turned into silent expectations?

Across the city, in his lonely hotel room, Kiran lay staring at the ceiling fan. The glow of his laptop cast shadows across his face. He was supposed to finish slides for tomorrow's review — but his mind was elsewhere.

Tara's voice from that Sunday call... it wouldn't leave him.

That dream she had. The boy who called her Amma.

And how much it shook her — more than she'd said out loud.

He hated how easily time slipped between them these days. How quickly small fights turned into silences. How he sometimes missed her messages, not because he didn't care, but because he didn't know how to respond without sounding tired.

He opened his gallery and scrolled back — photos of Tara in messy buns, blurry selfies of their late-night chats, a video of her laughing at his accent when drunk . His heart ached.

> ➢ "We didn't fall out of love," he whispered to no one. "We just forgot how to stay inside it."

That night, they both tried calling each other at the same time.

Tara's phone showed "Kiran calling…"

Kiran's screen read "Tara calling…"

They laughed, finally connecting.

"I was just thinking of you," she said.

"I never stopped," he replied.

The call was short — but it held something powerful. A softness. A knowing. A recognition that they were trying.

And sometimes, trying is a form of love.

➢ When did we forget us?

Maybe not in a moment… but in all the little ones we let pass.

But love, if true, always finds its way back — even through the smallest doors.

Chapter 9

Between Two Flights

The house was unusually quiet. A full week of holidays stretched ahead of Tara like a blank page — no office calls, no alarms, no excuse to be distracted. It should've felt peaceful. But instead, it made the silence feel louder.

She opened the cupboard to pull out some bedsheets and saw a small travel bag tucked in the corner — the one Kiran used whenever they traveled together. She touched the handle gently, and something inside her stirred.

Almost on impulse, she opened her laptop and checked flights.

There was one — early next morning. Just three hours to Kiran's city. No agenda. No warning. Just… her heart telling her to go.

She booked it.

Later that evening, she called him casually.

"So… the temple you mentioned last time — the one you never visited even though it's right there?"

"Yeah, what about it?" Kiran asked, flipping through documents.

"Wanna go tomorrow?"

There was a pause. "Tara…?"

"I'll be there by 7 a.m."

The line went quiet, and then he laughed — the kind of surprised, giddy laugh that came out only when he was truly caught off guard.

"You're serious?"

"Completely. I packed two kurtas. Don't expect miracles."

He was already checking maps for temple routes. "I'll pick you up."

The next morning, at the small airport terminal, Kiran spotted her even before she stepped out.

She looked travel-weary, hair in a loose braid, eyes sleepy but smiling. He stood there, awkward and excited, like a teenager on his first date.

"You really came," he said.

"I really needed to."

They didn't hug. They didn't hold hands.
But they smiled like people who had been
underwater too long and finally broke the
surface.

The drive to the temple was slow and quiet.
A small village road lined with neem trees,
sleepy vendors, and old houses that leaned
into each other like secrets.

They reached just before noon. The temple
wasn't grand — just a small, serene space
with age in its walls and peace in its air. The
priest was kind. The silence was kinder.

Tara lit a lamp.

She closed her eyes and didn't ask for
anything specific.

Just strength. And maybe… softness.

Kiran didn't say a word but stood beside her
the whole time, letting his silence speak
what he couldn't form into prayer.

After the darshan, they sat on the temple
steps, drinking sweet lime juice from paper
cups.

"You remember our first trip after marriage?" she asked.

"You mean the one where you lost your sandal in the river?"

She laughed. "Still your fault."

They talked. Lightly. Slowly. About nothing and everything.

And for the first time in a long time, it didn't feel like catching up. It felt like... continuing.

Before they headed back, Kiran stopped at a roadside shop and bought a pair of glass bangles — green ones. The vendor wrapped them gently and handed them to Tara.

"For you," he said, almost shy.

"I don't wear bangles much."

"I know. But you looked at them like you wanted to."

She didn't argue. She slipped them on.

And they glinted in the sun — delicate, yet whole.

> Love doesn't always arrive with music or milestones.

Sometimes it comes quietly — through unspoken prayers, temple bells, and the sound of green glass touching skin.

Chapter 10

The Language of Eyes

They reached Kiran's apartment late in the afternoon, sunlight filtering in like a gentle welcome. The air was warm, the room cluttered — a stack of unfolded laundry on the chair, a week's worth of dishes soaking in the sink, and the faint smell of instant noodles still lingering.

Tara chuckled, dropping her bag inside.

"This is how you've been living?" she teased, lifting a sock with two fingers.

Kiran scratched the back of his head, sheepish. "I was... uh, waiting for divine intervention."

"Great. God sent me instead."

What followed wasn't planned. But it felt right.

They cleaned together — not because it was romantic, but because it reminded them of older days. Kiran swept the balcony while Tara folded clothes and playfully mocked his color choices. She found one of her old hairbands in the drawer — a soft ache settled in her chest, but she tucked it away with a smile.

In the kitchen, they moved with quiet ease. Tara, who once struggled to even boil water, was now stirring sambhar like she'd been doing it all her life. Kiran prepped vegetables, his sleeves rolled up, humming some random tune off-key.

"Smells like home," he said, leaning in to sniff.

"Careful. I still remember how you almost sneezed into the rasam that one time."

They both laughed. It was easy —
dangerously easy — to slip back into them.

By the time evening settled in, the house was
cleaner, the dining table full, and their hearts
a little lighter.

They sat cross-legged on the floor, plates
between them, the television playing in the
background.

"India's playing today," Kiran said, already
reaching for the remote.

Tara groaned. "Of course."

But this time, she didn't argue. Instead, she
brought the dessert out, placed it in front of
him, and sat beside him with a soft smile.

They watched together — she asked
questions she already knew the answers to,
he explained anyway, eyes lit up like a child.

The match went on for hours. So did their soft chatter, casual teasing, and laughter.

Kiran glanced at her in the middle of the match. She was leaning back, eyes on the screen, content.

"Thanks for today," he said.

"For cleaning your mess?"

"For... reminding me what this place could feel like."

Tara didn't answer, but her eyes did.

Later that night, she stood by the window, watching the city lights shimmer. Kiran came beside her, holding two mugs of hot water.

"We didn't talk much about serious stuff today," she said quietly.

"Sometimes we don't need to," he replied. "Sometimes cleaning the house together says more than words."

She looked up at him. "You're right."

➢   Love is not always loud.

Sometimes it lives in the clatter of cleaned dishes.

In the way someone cuts vegetables just the way you like.

In the cricket scores read aloud to someone who doesn't even care.

In quiet evenings, after shared meals, where nothing is said — but everything is known.

As the night grew still, they didn't speak of tomorrow.

For now, today was enough.

Chapter 11

Kiranam – The Ray of Light

The rain tapped softly against the window.

Tara sat on the floor of Kiran's living room, wrapping her hands around a warm steel tumbler of coffee. The power had gone out for a while, leaving them in candlelight, surrounded by quiet and the scent of wet earth.

It felt like a moment asking to be remembered.

Kiran walked in with a blanket and sat across from her. He looked at her for a moment before speaking.

"Can I ask you something?"

She nodded, unsure.

"Do you ever feel… like you've failed?" His voice was low, careful, but honest.

Tara looked down at her coffee, tears threatening to blur her sight.

"Every day," she said. "Especially when people ask why we don't have children… when I see friends with their babies… when

I walk past the empty second bedroom in my flat.”

He listened — really listened.

“I used to think,” she continued, “that I had to be okay. That if I cried or got angry or doubted us, I’d break something precious. So I held it all in.”

Kiran moved closer. “I saw that. And I hated myself for not knowing how to help.”

She looked up, her voice trembling. “Why didn’t we talk about it? Really talk?”

“Because I was afraid too,” he admitted. “I thought if I said it out loud — that maybe it won’t happen for us — it would make it real. And I didn't want you to think I loved you any less if we never became parents.”

Tara let the words settle between them.

“I never needed you to fix it, Kiran,” she said softly. “I just needed you to sit beside me in the dark.”

Kiran’s eyes shimmered. “I’m sorry I didn’t know that sooner.”

There was silence.

But this time, it wasn't empty.

It was healing.

After a long pause, Tara whispered, "I had a name. For the child I dreamed of."

Kiran looked at her gently.

"She never came… but in my dreams, I called her Kiranam. My little ray of light."

Kiran swallowed hard, moved beyond words. "That's beautiful."

"She made me feel close to you… even when we were far."

He reached out then — not with words, but with a hand, steady and warm. She held it, and in that grip, years of silence melted.

"What do we do now?" she asked.

"We begin again," he said. "And this time, we don't walk alone."

They didn't make big decisions that night. No promises about IVF or adoption or plans.

But they made one quiet vow — to hold each other, whatever tomorrow held.

> Sometimes, healing doesn't come through
answers or outcomes.

It comes through presence. Through being
seen, heard, and held.

Through the quiet strength of love that
doesn't fix, but stays.

And in that staying, it becomes light — a ray
of hope. A Kiranam.

Chapter 12

Home is Us

It had been a month since Tara's spontaneous visit.

She stayed.

Not because everything was fixed — but because something had finally shifted.

The apartment looked a little different now. A new curtain she had picked. A corner with potted plants. The second bedroom, once silent and untouched, had a small bookshelf now — filled with poetry, photo frames, and quiet hope.

That morning, Tara woke up to the smell of ginger tea and the sound of Kiran humming tunelessly from the kitchen. She walked in groggily, watching him burn two toasts without realizing.

"Still the same terrible cook," she teased.

He turned, grinning. "Good morning to my favourite food critic."

She laughed, leaning against the counter.

Later that day, they sat in the balcony — a Sunday ritual now. Two cups of tea, one newspaper, and no rush.

They spoke of things gently — about checking with a fertility specialist again, about attending a yoga class together.

But they also spoke of what was now more important:

Planting a small garden.

Planning a weekend trek.

Finishing that puzzle they never opened.

And in between all that, they spoke of nothing.

Just silence. Just presence.

At one point, Tara leaned her head on his shoulder. "I used to think we had to achieve something to feel complete — a baby, a big home, some perfect picture."

Kiran nodded, listening.

"But I think... home is this," she said quietly. "You. Me. Tea on Sundays. Peace."

He didn't reply with words. He simply wrapped his arm around her.

> ➤ Not all love stories end with a baby's cry or a grand wedding.

Some end with laughter in small apartments, with mismatched mugs, and two people choosing each other — again and again.

They may still try. Maybe IVF. Maybe adoption. Maybe a surprise.

But that was no longer the definition of their worth.

Because the truest home was never a place or a child.

It was a decision.

To stay.

To try.

To love.

And to begin again.

As the sun dipped behind the buildings, casting a warm glow through the balcony railings, Tara whispered, "I'm not afraid anymore."

Kiran smiled, brushing a strand of hair behind her ear. "Neither am I."

And as they sat there — no longer chasing something distant, but resting in what was — they finally understood.

Home was not somewhere else.

Home... was them.

 THE END

About the Author

Gayathri is a passionate writer who believes in weaving emotions through ordinary lives. With a deep love for fiction rooted in real experiences, Tara Kiranam marks her one of her heartfelt writings

Based in South India, she draws inspiration from quiet conversations, warm silences, and the beauty of imperfect relationships. When not writing, she enjoys journaling, soulful music, and long walks under cloudy skies.

Author's Note

When I first began writing Tara Kiranam,
I wasn't sure where the story would go.
But I knew what I wanted it to feel like —
raw, soft, and honest.

If this story made you pause, reflect, cry,
or smile... then it's done what it was
meant to do.

Thank you for holding Tara and Kiran in
your heart. They are fragments of all of us
— trying, breaking, healing, and choosing
love anyway.

-Gayathri Reddy Yellamula